CAT AND DOG

by Else Holmelund Minarik

Pictures by Fritz Siebel

SCHOLASTIC INC.

New York Toronto London Auckland Sydney Tokyo

This book belongs to

_____

ISBN 0-590-09895-0

23 22 21 20 19 18 17 16 15 14 13 12   5 6 7 8 9/8 0/9

Printed in the U.S.A.   07

CAT AND DOG

"Woof! Woof!

Off the bed,

Cat, Cat,

"Or I'll make

A catball out of you,

I will, I will."

"Meow, meow,

I'll get off,

I will, I will."

"Woof! Woof!

Off the chair,

Cat, Cat,

"Or I'll make

A catcoat out of you,

I will, I will."

"Meow, meow,

I'll get off,

I will, I will."

"Woof! Woof!

Off the table,

Cat, Cat,

"Or I'll make

A catpie out of you,

I will, I will."

"Meow, meow,

Come and get me,

Dog, Dog,

If you can,

If you can."

"Here! Here!

Off the table,

Silly Dog,

Silly Cat.

"Animals on the table!

My goodness!

The very idea."

"Meow—Meow—

Out of the water,

Dog, Dog.

You will make the house wet,

You will, you will."

"Woof! Woof!

Here I come.

Here I come."

"Meow—Meow—

Out of the garden,

Dog, Dog.

You will be tied up—

You will, you will."

"Woof! Woof!

Here I come.

I am coming."

"Meow—Meow—

Here are bones,

Dog, Dog.

Get them out.

Get them out."

"Woof! Woof!

Bones for me

—and for you.

Bones for us."

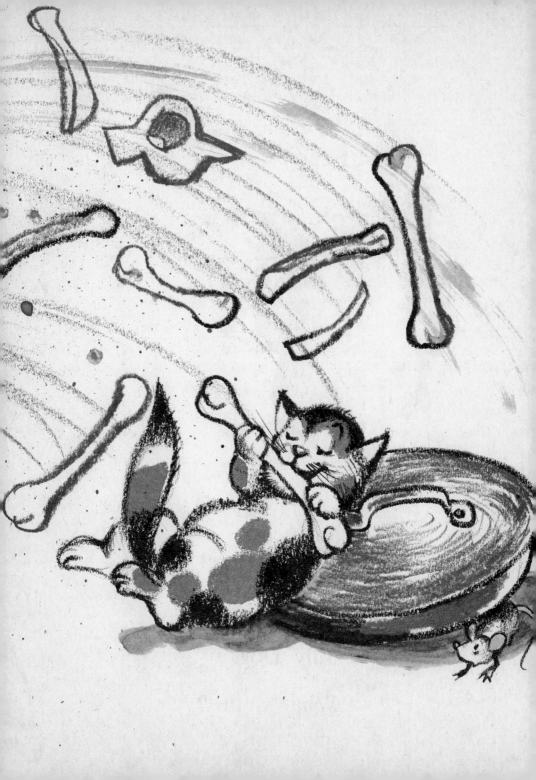

"Here! Here!

Silly Cat.

Silly Dog.

What is this?

"Are you so hungry?

Well, then,

I will feed you.

"Are you happy now?

Good."